Let's Go for a Ride

MAXWELL NEWHOUSE

Tundra Books

Published in Canada by Tundra Books,
481 University Avenue, Toronto, Ontario M5G 2E9

Published in the United States by Tundra Books of Northern New York,
P.O. Box 1030, Plattsburgh, New York 12901

Library of Congress Control Number: 2005923898

Library and Archives Canada Cataloguing in Publication

Newhouse, Maxwell
        Let's go for a ride / Maxwell Newhouse.

ISBN 0-88776-748-6

        1. Automobiles – Juvenile literature. 2. Drive-in facilities – Juvenile
literature. I. Title.

TL147.N49 2005   j629.222   C2005-901733-3

We acknowledge the financial support of the Government of Canada through the Book Publishing Industry Development Program (BPIDP) and that of the Government of Ontario through the Ontario Media Development Corporation's Ontario Book Initiative. We further acknowledge the support of the Canada Council for the Arts and the Ontario Arts Council for our publishing program.

ONTARIO ARTS COUNCIL
CONSEIL DES ARTS DE L'ONTARIO

Medium: Oil on canvas

Printed in China

1 2 3 4 5 6   11 10 09 08 07 06

To my sons, James and Jonathen

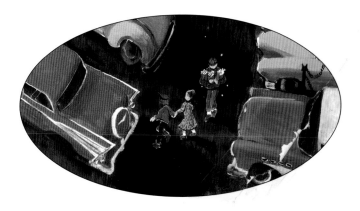

ACKNO'. LEDGMENTS

Thank you to Barrie Mowatt of the Buschlen Mowatt Gallery
for his continuing support.
A.. a special thank-you to the staff and students
of the F.G. Leary Elementary School in Chilliwack, B.C.

*T*hey made strange noises. They belched smoke. They frightened the meek and thrilled the brave. In the late 1800s, most people thought the newfangled "self-propelled motor vehicles" wouldn't last. Boy, were they wrong! For all their noise and danger, their smoke and smog, my heart still skips a beat when somebody says, "Let's go for a ride!"

*I*n the early days, cars shared the unpaved roads with horses and wagons.
Families who could afford cars joined automobile clubs and had group outings
just for fun. Unfortunately, there were few places to buy gasoline, so people often
ran out of gas and had to walk home. Some even had to get a horse to pull their car!

*F*inding a gas or filling station along the roadside became a necessity of life.
By 1905, curbside gasoline pumps were part of the General Store.
But in 1912, they were replaced by small service stations that sold only gasoline.

With gasoline now readily available, the automobile crowd
began to enjoy camping along roadways in the countryside.
This was the start of the camping many of us do today.

*N*ew jobs sprang up to accommodate the car and its passengers. Hungry travelers would stop at small roadside stands, place their order, and young folk would carry the refreshments to the vehicles. This made it quick and easy to get on the road again. Today, these fast-food outlets are often part of gas stations and rest stops.

People and cars: it was love from the start. In 1933, a man had an idea – why not enjoy a
movie in the privacy of your own car? He fastened a bedsheet between two trees, and projected
a film from the hood of his car onto the sheets. This was the birth of the drive-in theater.
It seemed that automobile owners wanted to do everything in the comfort of their cars.

Camp cabins, or roadside auto courts, were built for weary travelers. These small cabins, or cottages, had a sleeping area, private washroom, and cooking facilities. The auto courts were designed in a horseshoe shape, with a children's play area in the center. They were often located by rivers or streams and many families considered them a dream vacation spot.

Car owners who wanted to cross rivers or inlets had to share the small ferries with horses and wagons. The ferries became so crowded that it wasn't long before this type of transportation had to change, and larger vessels were employed to carry all the traffic.

As the years passed, the roads became crowded with vehicles of different sizes, shapes, and types. Some people wanted to get more belongings into their cars and still have room to sleep. Cars and trucks with campers, travel trailers, and tent trailers became the rage, and so did campgrounds to hold them all.

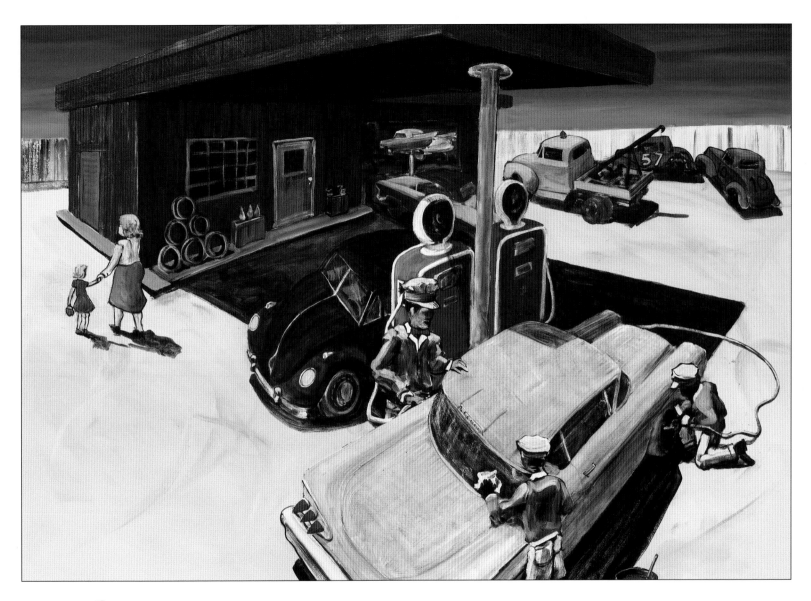

*T*he single pump in front of the corner store gave way to fancy streamlined service stations, known as gas stations. Attendants in snappy uniforms filled your car with gas, checked fluid levels, tires, and oil, washed your windows and sometimes even your whole car. Most service stations offered mechanics that kept your automobile in tip-top form, and made your ride a smooth one.

*E*very year brought new car models with snazzy fresh colors, modern shapes, and the latest and greatest gadgets. New car dealerships were popping up everywhere, and used-car sales rocketed. Jobs were plentiful in the auto industry and just about everyone could afford a car.

Going for a ride wasn't just a matter of having fun getting there. People wanted to get there fast! As long as there were wheels on it, any car could join the race. Old cars, ready to be discarded, were called jalopies. These cars would be put on a racetrack and raced, until they were smashed or simply unable to run anymore.

Racing soon became a North American pastime. Children began to build wooden racecars with whatever they could find. They would use old wooden crates and even the boxes soap came in. Then they would attach any type of wheel they had.

A prize was given to the first soapbox car to finish the race.
Soapbox racing started in 1933 in the United States, and soon spread to Canada,
Mexico, and South Africa. Today it is known as a soapbox derby.

Before long there were many cars that no one wanted or needed. Some ended up on used-car lots and some joined the piles of scrap metal in the junkyards. Large cranes piled them high in the air, on top of each other, to rust out or be used for parts.

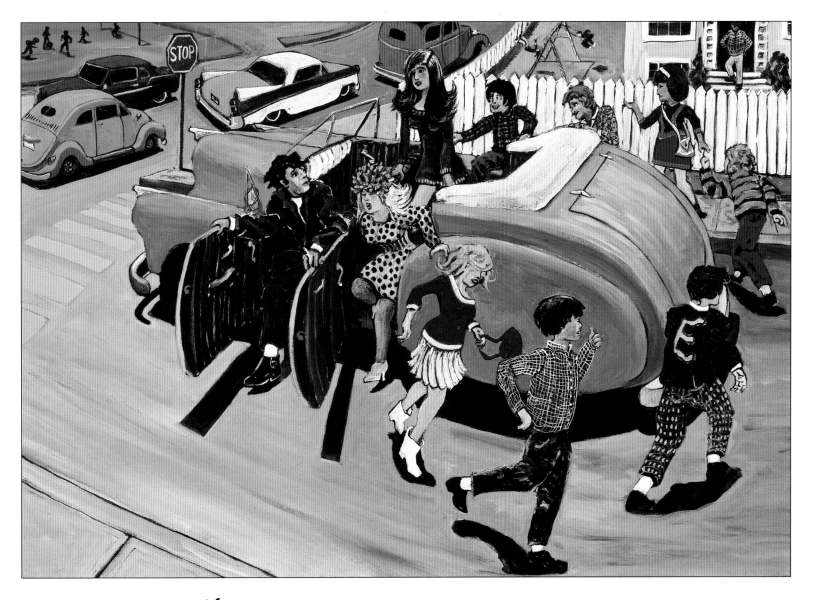

Young people could buy these old cars very inexpensively.
Sometimes they turned them into hotrods, or racing cars;
other times they just drove around in them for fun.

We were beginning to take our cars for granted. We used our cars to travel in, work in, play in, and even eat in. Why get dressed up to go out for dinner, when you could eat in the privacy of your own car?

Drive-in restaurants became the latest craze.
A carhop would come out, take your order, then bring
the food to your vehicle, so you could sit back and enjoy.

By the 1950s, cars were said to be in their "glory days."
The bigger the better,
with no worry about fuel restrictions or engine size.

Rock and roll music, drive-in movies,
fast food, and a great car:
life was good.

Cars still make strange noises and now that there are so many of them,
it's alarming how much smoke they can belch out,
but we love them all the same. These days I walk whenever I can,
and I often ride my bike. I keep my car for those times
when we get together for family fun, and somebody says,
"It's a beautiful day!

Let's go for a ride."